Zidar

Tio

Shadow

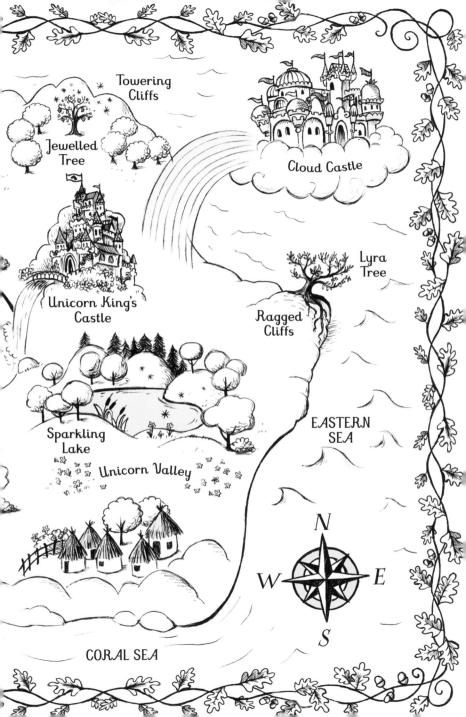

Contents

Chapter One

Zoe crept out of her Great Aunt May's house, closing the door quietly behind her.

The night was warm, with a light breeze rustling the dry grasses. It was the end of the summer holidays, and the end of summer too – Zoe could sense it in the air as she made her way to the bottom of the garden and stood beneath the old oak tree.

Its branches were silhouetted against the starry sky, its great trunk wider, even, than Zoe's outstretched arms. She smiled, for between its roots was a magical path that led to Unicorn Island.

Zoe knew this would be her last visit to the island for a long time. Soon, she'd be back at home, and getting ready to go to school again.

She gazed up at the branches for a moment, then reached for her tiny pouch of magic dust. Sprinkling it over herself, she chanted the words of a spell:

Let me pass into the magic tree,
Where *fairy* unicorns *fly* wild and *free*.
Show me the trail of sparkling light,
To Unicorn Island, shining bright.

At once, Zoe felt that familiar, magical, tingling feeling, and then she was shrinking, *down, down, down,* until she was fairy-sized, small enough to enter the tunnel between the writhing roots of the oak tree.

She ran down the tunnel, her heart beating with excitement at the thought of entering her secret world. At last, she rounded a corner, and saw a glimmer of light, and beyond it, the Silvery Glade.

"Oh!" gasped Zoe, as she entered the glade, her breath taken away by the wonder of it all.

The air was soft and damp, a gentle mist curling around the silvered trees. The fallen rainbow leaves lay strewn across the woodland floor, crunching softly under her bare feet.

Then came the sound of pounding hooves and Astra, her best friend on Unicorn Island, was galloping towards her, the stars on her back shining through the mist.

Zoe flung her arms around Astra's neck and breathed in the warm, honey scent of her.

"I'm so glad you're back," said Astra.

"Oh! Me too," said Zoe. "It's wonderful to be here again."

"The Unicorn King is in the forest too," said Astra, "just beyond the glade. He's visiting my mother. Would you like to come and see him, while he's here?"

Zoe nodded, and Astra bent her legs so Zoe could swing herself onto her back. Then they raced together through the trees, rainbow leaves flying up beneath Astra's beating hooves.

"So, what's happened since I've been away?" asked Zoe.

"Well…" Astra began. "The King has set Shadow free!"

"Really?" gasped Zoe.

Shadow was a fairy pony, who had long been trying to take over Unicorn Island. When he had finally been defeated, the King had Shadow locked away in a cage of vines, then guarded on a far-flung island. It was strange to think of him roaming free.

"I know," said Astra. "The King has decided Shadow's no longer a threat to us. He thinks Shadow is truly sorry for everything he did. But no one has seen Shadow since or knows where he's gone."

"I really hope the King is right," said Zoe. She paused a moment before speaking again, remembering what else she had learnt on her last visit. The King had told Astra that one day she could become a Guardian – one of the powerful unicorns who helped to care for Unicorn Island. But first, to prove herself, Astra had to do three things to help the island, and in ways that showed exceptional magic.

"You've passed two of the tests to become a Guardian now," said Zoe, speaking her thoughts aloud. "Together we found the Grimoire and the Silver Chalice. That means you've only got one more challenge left."

She expected Astra to tell her of her next plan, or at least to seem excited, but instead Astra's brow was creased with worry.

"What is it?" asked Zoe. "What's the matter?

Has something happened?"

Astra glanced over at her, as Zoe slid from her back. "I'll tell you later," she whispered. "The King is just around the corner."

They walked the last part of the way, along a winding stream and over a little wooden bridge. On the other side, Zoe could see the King and Astra's mother, Sorrel, deep in discussion. But as soon as they saw Astra and Zoe they stopped talking, looked up and smiled.

"Welcome back to Unicorn Island, Zoe," said Sorrel, beaming at her.

"It's wonderful to have you with us again," added the King. "I'm doing my yearly tour of the island. This morning, it's the turn of Fairtree Forest."

Zoe had to keep smiling in order to hide her shock. The King looked so different to the last time she had seen him – frailer and smaller, somehow. His golden horn no longer gleamed and his coat was dull and lacklustre.

"What's happened to him?" she wondered to herself. "It wasn't that long since I last saw him. Why is he so changed?"

But she said nothing, just nodded and chatted until the King said it was time for him to leave.

"I have to go to the Flower Meadows next, before returning to the castle for a meeting of the Guardians." Then he turned to Sorrel. "Thank you," he said, "for all your hard work in looking after the trees and woodland creatures. It's been wonderful to see nature flourishing in the forest under your care."

The King smiled at them one last time, then stretched out his wide gossamer wings and rose up through the branches, before disappearing above the treetops.

Once he'd left, Zoe couldn't hold in her worries any longer.

"Is the King...unwell?" she asked.

"I've been worried about him, too," said Astra. "Is there something the matter with him, Mother?"

"The King isn't ill," Sorrel replied. "I think he's coming to the end of his reign."

"The end of his reign?" queried Zoe. "What does that mean?"

"Being ruler of Unicorn Island is a difficult task," explained Sorrel. "The King has been ruling for many years, and the battle with Shadow has been long and hard. When a unicorn has used so much of his or her magic, they become weaker...frailer. This may have been happening for some time, but the King will have used his magic to hide it."

"Oh!" said Zoe. "Can't one of the Guardians take over so the King can rest, at least for a while?"

"It doesn't work like that," Sorrel explained gently. "The King can only pass on the crown when the next unicorn – male or female, young or old – shows themselves as fit to rule over Unicorn Island."

"How can he tell who that is?" asked Zoe. "Do you already know who it will be?"

"It's revealed by a magical sign," said Sorrel, "written in our Book of Prophecies, which only the ruler of Unicorn Island is allowed to see. But don't worry about the King," Sorrel continued. "I'm sure the new ruler will show themselves soon. And as soon as the King has rested, he will heal."

Zoe tried to take in what Sorrel was saying, but the thought of someone ruling in the King's place just felt wrong.

"I had better leave you now," said Sorrel. "I must look after the woodland rabbits. Some of them are upset over their flooded burrows and I want to help them find new homes.

After that, I must join the meeting of the Guardians at the castle. Zoe, if I don't see you again, have a wonderful time on the island."

Zoe waved goodbye to Sorrel and, as soon as she was out of earshot, Astra began speaking again.

"I've been thinking about my third challenge," she said. "I just didn't want to mention it until we were alone together. This is the challenge that could make me a Guardian...and it's one that I hope will help the King."

"That sounds brilliant," said Zoe, her eyes lighting up. "Maybe if we can find a way to help the King, he won't have to give up the crown yet."

"There's just one problem..." said Astra.

"It could be dangerous."

Zoe had to laugh. "Astra!" she said. "When has that ever stopped us before?"

Then she saw Astra's expression, and gulped. "Oh my goodness," she said. "I've never seen you look so serious. Tell me – what's your idea?"

Astra cleared her throat. "I've been reading in the castle library again," she said, "and I found a book about a magical ball, known as the Golden Orb. The books says that whoever possesses the Orb gains incredible strength – and that's just what the King needs."

"Now I have to ask…" said Zoe. "What's the dangerous part?"

Astra cast a spell and, a moment later,
a map appeared in the air above them,
surrounded by sparkles.

"I read that the Golden Orb is kept on
the Floating Islands, a group of tiny islands
which sit high in the sky, far above
Unicorn Island. Look..." she added, pointing
at the map.

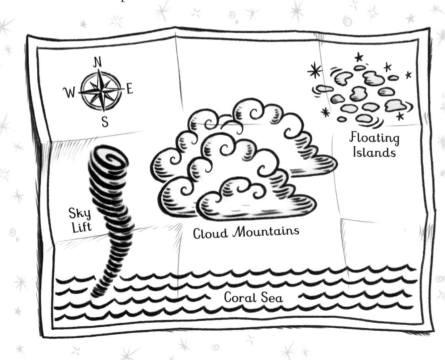

"To reach the islands, we'll have to fly across the Coral Sea, and then ride the Sky Lift."

"And from there," said Zoe, tracing a path with her finger, "we keep flying east, through the Cloud Mountains until we reach the Floating Islands." Zoe looked over at Astra. "What makes you think this will be dangerous?"

"It said in the book..." said Astra, her voice dropping to a whisper, "...that no one who has been to the Floating Islands has ever come back."

Zoe gasped.

"Did you show the Guardians the map? Have you asked them about it?"

"About what?" came a voice.

Astra quickly cast a spell and the map faded from view. Then both Zoe and Astra turned to see their friend, Tio, trotting towards them through the woods. As usual, his saddlebags were bursting full of spell books, his mane was a mess and his round-rimmed glasses were askew.

"Nothing!" said Astra, quickly.

"I don't believe that for a moment," said Tio. "You two must be planning one of your adventures again."

"Do you want to come with us?" teased Zoe, knowing that Tio loved nothing more than staying safe within the castle walls, reading his spell books.

"I vowed not to go on any more quests with you two, and I meant it," said Tio, grinning. "Besides, I've an important mission today. I'm looking for a very particular wild flower in the woods for a spell."

"Good luck finding it," said Astra.

"Hmm," said Tio. "I'll be on my way then. Even though I know you two are *definitely* up to something."

He trotted past them, heading deeper into the woods, then stopped and turned. "But if you do get into trouble, you know I'd come and help, don't you?"

"I know," said Astra, smiling at him. "Thank you, Tio."

Astra waited until Tio had disappeared

between the trees. "I didn't want to drag Tio into this," she said, "and I haven't told the Guardians anything as they'll say it's too dangerous. So if we set out to find the Golden Orb, no one will know where we've gone. But I think this a risk worth taking. What do you think, Zoe?"

"I agree," said Zoe. "The King really needs our help. He'd never ask us to take a risk for him, but he deserves it, after all that he's done for the island."

Astra grinned. "Then climb on my back, Zoe. Let the adventure begin..."

Chapter Two

In one swift motion, Zoe swung herself onto
Astra's back and they began galloping out of
Fairtree Forest. Near the southern tip, where
the trees ended in a line of gentle hills, Astra
beat her glimmering wings until they were
soaring up and up, into the misty blue.

Zoe smiled; her eyes shone. Nothing ever
beat the excitement of flying. The gentle

breeze brushed against her cheeks and ruffled her hair. And as they flew, she tried to ignore the niggle of worry that this might just be their most dangerous mission yet.

Astra kept flying south, the morning sun shimmering through the clouds, until they reached the shores of the Coral Sea.

"Oh wow!" said Zoe, looking down. "I've never been this far south before."

As the mists cleared, she could see that the waters were crystal clear, with coral

blooming across the sea floor in intricate, swirling patterns.

"Have you ever taken the Sky Lift before?" Zoe asked as they flew.

"Never," Astra replied. "I've heard other unicorns talk about it though. It sounds almost like a fairground ride! It's a funnel of wind and, when you enter it, you're sucked up into the sky, higher and higher, so you can reach the skies far above Unicorn Island."

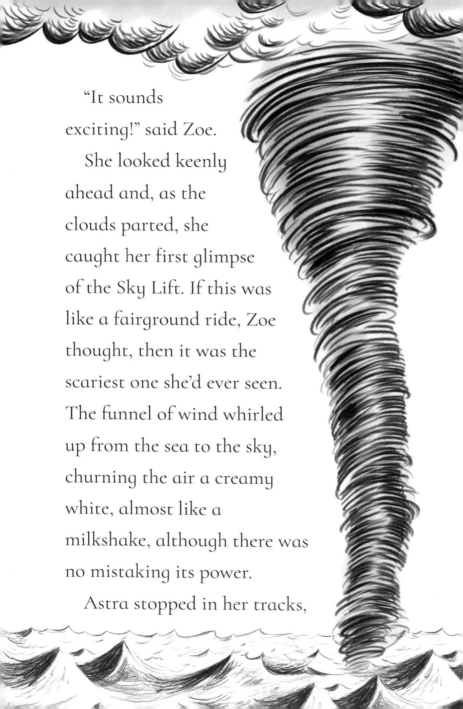

"It sounds exciting!" said Zoe.

She looked keenly ahead and, as the clouds parted, she caught her first glimpse of the Sky Lift. If this was like a fairground ride, Zoe thought, then it was the scariest one she'd ever seen. The funnel of wind whirled up from the sea to the sky, churning the air a creamy white, almost like a milkshake, although there was no mistaking its power.

Astra stopped in her tracks,

her beating wings keeping them suspended in the air.

"That looks...terrifying!" said Zoe. "Do you think that's the reason no one makes it back from the Floating Islands?"

Astra shook her head. "The Sky Lift isn't meant to be dangerous...just fast, at least from what I've heard about it."

"Is there any other way to get to the Floating Islands?" asked Zoe.

"Only if we fly ourselves, but that could take all day," said Astra. "And then I'll be exhausted when we get there, and we don't know what dangers lie ahead."

"Then let's take the Sky Lift," said Zoe determinedly, steeling herself against her rising sense of fear.

Astra nodded and began powering through the air. The closer they got to the Sky Lift, the louder the whirling noise became. Zoe could see the wind spiralling up through the tunnel while its roaring sound filled her ears.

"Are you ready?" asked Astra, when they reached the edge of the tunnel. She had to shout to make her voice heard.

"I'm ready!" Zoe shouted back.

"Then here goes!" said Astra. Zoe clung on tight and together they plunged into the tunnel of wind.

At once, Zoe felt her breath being sucked away as they began spinning and whooshing upwards through the tunnel. Zoe clung tighter still to Astra, her arms around Astra's neck, hands clasped, fingers tightly laced, terrified she might be pulled away at any moment.

Zoe tried to call out to Astra, to make sure she was okay, but her voice was whipped away. She grew more and more dizzy, until it seemed to Zoe as if the whole world was spinning and as if the roaring in her ears would never stop.

And then, all of a sudden, they reached the top of the Sky Lift. With a great WHOOSH! they were shot up into the sky, free of the noise and the whirling.

Zoe opened her eyes to see blue skies, with no sign of sea or land below them, as if they'd been spun from the Sky Lift into another world. Around them hung huge, white fluffy clouds, blooming like marshmallow flowers.

"That was...amazing!" said Zoe, giddy with relief that they'd made it. "I think maybe the Sky Lift is like a fairground ride, after all."

"The fastest fairground ride *ever*," said Astra, grinning, stretching out her wings so they hovered for a moment, taking it all in. "Phew! I think my mind has only just stopped spinning."

"Mine too," Zoe replied. "But I wonder which way it is now. The map said we need to keep flying east, towards the Cloud Mountains, but I don't even know which way that is anymore! I feel lost up here..."

Astra swivelled around. "This way," she said, confidently, nodding her horn.

"How do you know?" asked Zoe.

Astra paused for a moment before answering. "I'm not sure," she said. "It's as if I have a compass in my head. I always know which way is north or south or west or east, even on cloudy days when I can't work it out by the sun."

"Well I'm glad at least one of us knows," said Zoe, "because I'd be lost on my own." She kept her voice light-hearted but, inside, she couldn't help wishing she was more like Astra – so capable, and so full of magic.

As they flew on through the airy blue, Zoe's worries about their adventure began to fade. It was so beautiful up here, flying among the clouds, the sun shining down on them and the rest of the world suddenly so far away, as if no more than a dream.

"Magical," Zoe whispered beneath her breath, feeling so lucky to be here, right now, flying on Astra's back.

"We just need to find the Cloud Mountains," said Astra, "and then the Floating Islands shouldn't be far beyond."

Zoe peered into the distance, shielding her eyes from the glow of the sun. "Oh look!" she said. "Up ahead! Towering mountain-shaped clouds! Aren't they amazing?"

"They're beautiful!" said Astra. "Like

something from a painting. Somehow, I'd imagined they'd be white though, not dark."

"Perhaps they're just silhouetted against the sun?" suggested Zoe. "Although there seem to be strange flashes of light around them, too. I can't work out where they're coming from."

Astra put on a burst of speed and flew towards the Cloud Mountains, eager to reach them, her gossamer wings beating, her pearly horn glowing in the sunlight.

But as they drew closer, Zoe realized these mountains were like nothing she had ever seen at home – or even on Unicorn Island. They were huge and dark, like thunder clouds. Every now and then they sparked out angry bolts of lightning, which zigzagged through the sky. And inside each cloud were swirling icy hailstones, each one the size

of a boulder.

"Oh, Astra!" said Zoe. "Those mountains look terrifying!"

"And that's not all," said Astra. "Look, Zoe! I think...they're moving!"

Astra and Zoe watched, open-mouthed, as the Cloud Mountains sped towards each other, crashing together, sparking even bigger bolts of lightning. They came apart, only to crash together again, rumbling with fury. And all around them, the sky was growing dark...

Chapter Three

"And I thought the Sky Lift looked scary..." said Zoe, eyeing up the Cloud Mountains in trepidation. "How are we ever going to get through them? We can't fly around them. It looks as if they stretch on forever."

Astra was silent for a moment, simply watching the Cloud Mountains as they moved apart and came together, lightning flashing through the darkening skies.

"Is there a spell you can cast?" asked Zoe.

"I'm not sure," Astra replied, her brow furrowed. "I could try casting a protective bubble around us, but what if the force of the mountains is too much? We could be squashed flat!"

"Let's not take a chance on that!" said Zoe. "Could you stop the mountains from moving – just long enough for us to pass through?"

"I could try," said Astra. "It's going to take a huge amount of magic, but I'm not sure what else we can do..."

She was silent for a while, working out her spell, and then Astra bowed her head and began to chant:

Cloud Mountains, hear me!
Stop in your tracks.
Stay where you are and don't move back.
Let freezing winds hold you, keep you still,
Hear my spell and bow to my will.

As Astra spoke the words, the air around them began fizzing and crackling with magic, and the stars on Astra's back shone bright, glowing silver against her soft coat.

From Astra's pearly horn came a flurry of snowflakes that became a swirling, freezing wind, snaking its way towards the mountains, and covering them in a glittering layer of frost.

"I think it's working!" said Zoe. "Look! The mountains are freezing. They're stopping moving. Quick, Astra! Let's fly through them."

They began speeding towards the line of mountains, aiming for the narrow pass between the nearest two. But as they reached them, Zoe noticed the layer of frost starting to crack and splinter.

"Oh no!" Zoe cried. "Stop, Astra! I don't think the spell is holding!"

Astra reared up, just in time, as the frost shattered, filling the air with glittering shards of ice. Moments later, the mountains began rumbling and moving once more.

Astra turned and flew until they were a safe distance away. "These Cloud Mountains are an elemental force," she said, breathlessly. "My magic is never going to work against them. They're just too strong."

Zoe was thinking, hard.

"What if you work *with* them?" she said. "Is there some way to communicate with them? Or to slow them rather than freeze them?"

"Of course," said Astra, her face lighting up with a smile. "Why didn't I think of that? Thank you, Zoe."

And she bowed her head to cast a new spell...

Cloud Mountains, hear me! This time I ask,
    You slow your speed so we can pass...
Grow still! Grow quiet! Breathe in my balm,
    A moment of peace, when all is calm...

This time, when Astra bowed her horn, she sent out a warm wind, filled with petals and the sweet scent of wild flowers. And Zoe could tell that the mountains were listening. The hailstones stopped swirling in the thunderous clouds; there were no more sparks of lightning. The mountains slowed their movement to a faint crawl and she could feel a sense of calm, filling the air.

"Thank you!" Astra cried out to the Cloud Mountains. Then she took flight again, speeding between their towering peaks.

On and on they flew, the mountain chain seeming to stretch endlessly across the skies.

"I can see the end in sight!" cried Zoe, at last, pointing to the blue skies beyond the last of the peaks.

But even as they flew, the mountains began to move again, as if the enchantment was weakening.

Slowly, slowly, the Cloud Mountains were inching towards each other, the hail storms swirling, the clouds rumbling, and tiny sparks of lightning lit the air.

"Oh no!" said Zoe. "The spell is wearing off. Can you cast it again?"

But Astra shook her head. "I don't think it will work again," she said. "At least, not for a while. The Cloud Mountains are longing to return to their natural state. I can sense it."

Then she stopped speaking, to save her breath for the flight ahead. Zoe could see, to her horror, that the gap they needed to pass through was narrowing…

As they neared the end, Zoe called out. "You can do this, Astra!" she urged, willing her on. "We just need one last burst of speed."

Astra beat her wings even more furiously. Zoe crouched low over Astra, the wind whipping across her back, and with a great cry of relief they slipped through the last of the Cloud Mountains.

Zoe turned back, just in time to see the mountains crash together, the spell broken, the air filled with rumbling roars.

"You did it!" Zoe said, hugging Astra, closing her eyes in relief. "We're one step closer to finding the Golden Orb."

But Astra was staring dead ahead, her eyes wide. "The Floating Islands, Zoe..."

And Zoe, too, looked over and gasped.

Chapter Four

The Floating Islands lay just beyond the end
of the Cloud Mountains, suspended in the air
in a golden haze. Zoe thought they were the
most wonderful thing she had ever seen
– even more beautiful than Unicorn Island.

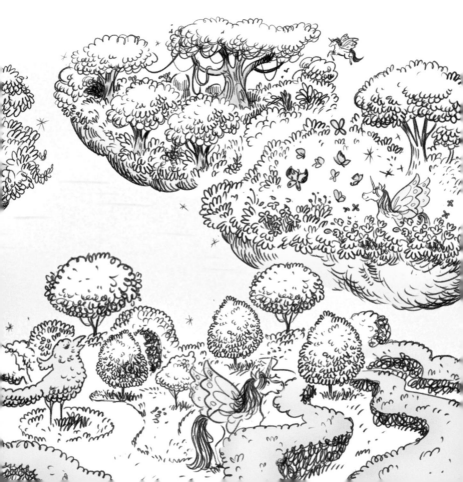

They landed on the nearest island and gazed out at the others. There were hundreds of them, each one tiny, but perfect, all bathed in a dazzling glow as they hovered together in the air, shimmering and sparkling. Some of the islands were covered in flowers, others were little watery havens, full of trickling streams and flowing fountains. Zoe spotted one that was lush and green, with gently swaying trees and blooming orchids. Another was covered in butterflies, their jewel-like wings glinting in the sun. Each island was tended by a fairy unicorn.

"What is this place?" Astra wondered aloud.

Before Zoe could answer, she saw a large unicorn, gleaming gold as the sun, swaggering out to greet them, fluttering his shiny wings.

"Welcome to the Floating Islands," he said. "My name is Zidar, but you can call me the Sky King, as I am the ruler here. How wonderful that you've  come to join us. Every unicorn that finds their way here receives a little island of their own to make and shape, just the way they want it."

Zoe looked over at Astra, to see her reaction. There was something at the back of her mind...something niggling. A question, perhaps, that she should be asking Zidar? Something to do with the reason they were here...but the harder Zoe tried to think, the foggier her mind became. And judging by Astra's confused expression, she felt just the same.

And as they stood there, wondering, the golden glow from the islands washed over them, bathing them in its light.

"What's going on?" Zoe asked Zidar. "This light...is it magical? I can't remember why we came..."

"There's nothing to worry about," Zidar replied smoothly. "Just follow me."

Zoe once again swung herself onto Astra's back and they followed Zidar through the sky.

"This one could be yours," he said, pointing to a little, empty island on his left.

"Thank you..." said Astra, as she fluttered across to it.

"Make of it what you wish," said Zidar. "For on these islands you will find your magic is far stronger than it was at home. Here, you will discover, you can make your dreams come true!"

Then Zidar called out, "Have fun!" as he sailed away on his golden wings.

"I can't remember what we're doing here," said Zoe. "Is this what we came here for? To create our own island?"

"I don't know," Astra stammered. "My mind feels all...foggy."

"Mine too," said Zoe. "Maybe we should

just do as Zidar suggests? He said everyone has more powers here. Do you think," Zoe went on, her heart beating fast at the thought, "that means I can do magic here?"

"You could try?" said Astra.

Zoe looked around their island. "I'd like a little shady grove of trees here," she said, pointing – and at once, exactly as she'd imagined it, five silvery trees appeared around the edge of the island, with fluttering rainbow leaves, just like the ones on Unicorn Island.

"Wow!" gasped Zoe. "I *can* do magic here! Astra, isn't that amazing? Now you try."

Astra smiled at Zoe's excitement. "I'd like a palace," she said, "made of sweets!"

In a shower of sparkles, a palace appeared in the middle of the island, with balustrades made of candy canes, and candy floss roofs.

Astra laughed with delight. "This is incredible!"

After that, Zoe and Astra went on adding to their island, conjuring up lollipop trees and a chocolate fountain, mountains of cakes and golden lakes, filled with shining

stars. The only limit was their imagination.

Time seemed to pass in a blur, and Zoe found she had no sense of morning or night. The golden glow was always the same, surrounding her in a daze of happiness.

"At last," she thought. "I'm like Astra. I can do magic, too! And even better than that, we're making something together."

But as Zoe smiled and pointed, making their island ever more fantastical, Astra felt a growing sense of unease.

"Something feels wrong," she said. "I just don't know what it is. But I keep wondering – how can everyone's magic be more powerful here than on Unicorn Island?

It doesn't make any sense."

"Does it matter?" said Zoe. "What's amazing is that at last, like you, I can do magic too. We should just enjoy it. Look, I've made a row of sherbert flowers. And next," she added, grinning, "I'm going to fill the lake with tiny, exploding marshmallows."

"Maybe you're right," said Astra. "We should just enjoy this..."

"Of course I'm right," said Zoe, bubbling over with happiness. "Let's stay here. FOREVER!"

But the word 'forever' made Astra freeze. "What was it the book said?" she asked herself. "Nobody ever comes back..." At those words, it was as if the golden glow that had been fogging her mind began to clear.

"Zoe," said Astra, urgently. "That's why nobody ever comes back from the Floating Islands. Because it's a trap!"

"That's exactly what it is," said a deep voice – a voice that Zoe and Astra knew only too well. They both turned to look and there, hovering above them in the golden sky, was...Shadow!

Chapter Five

For a moment, Zoe and Astra simply stared at the fairy pony in shock. The last time they had seen Shadow, the King and Magus had been taking him to a far-flung island, until he could prove he was no longer a threat to Unicorn Island.

"What are you doing here?" asked Astra.

"I've been released," said Shadow. "For

good behaviour. Didn't you know?"

"But why have you come *here*?" asked Astra. "Have you been following us?"

She looked over at Zoe as she spoke, and could see that Zoe's eyes were clearing, just as she felt the last of the fog lifting from her own mind.

"I expect I'm here for the same reason you are," said Shadow, sardonically. "I didn't follow you both, but I had a feeling I'd find you here. You came for the Golden Orb, didn't you?"

"Yes!" cried Astra. "That's it! That's why we're here!" She looked at Zoe. "Do you remember?" she asked, urgently.

Slowly, Zoe nodded.

"We did come here for that," she said, still

feeling very uncertain... "But I'm not sure we want it now. It's so wonderful here. I thought we could just stay..."

Shadow swooped down, so he was standing on their little floating island, towering over them. Zoe took a step back.

The King might have announced that Shadow

could now be trusted, but Zoe couldn't bring herself to believe it. Not after everything he'd put them through.

"I would have thought you'd both have the power to withstand Zidar's spell," Shadow drawled. "But I suppose you didn't realize what you were letting yourselves in for, did you?"

"Shadow, please," said Astra, impatiently. "Stop talking in riddles and tell us what's going on!"

"I can see you're not going to catch on by yourselves," sighed Shadow. "The Floating Islands are a trap, just as you said. Zidar uses the power of the Golden Orb to create an illusion of magic. Unicorns are drawn to the islands because they seem so beautiful.

Then he gets them to cast spell after spell to create their own little worlds. But for every spell a unicorn casts, Zidar steals their magic – he sucks it away, little by little. One day soon, he'll be even more powerful than the King, and I expect you can guess what will happen then…"

"What do you mean, it's all an illusion?" asked Zoe.

"All these islands," replied Shadow, "are no more than pieces of empty, floating rock. But Zidar has enchanted them, so as soon as you come near, you're caught by their spell. From that moment on, you only see what Zidar wants you to see."

"But then why hasn't it worked on you?" asked Astra.

"Because I have nothing to give," said Shadow, with a careless shrug. "I have no magic at all. The enchantment only seeks out those with  powers so Zidar can steal their magic. Otherwise, these islands would be full of all kinds of non-magical creatures."

"But Zidar's spell worked on me," said Zoe, shocked. "And I don't have any magic."

"You've felt that fizzing in your veins, haven't you?" said Shadow. "It's your connection to Astra. It means you have some of her magic. Not much," he sneered, "but enough."

"Why hasn't the Unicorn King stopped this?" asked Astra, puzzled. "Why hasn't he come for Zidar?"

Shadow gave a hollow laugh. "It's not as if the King lets me in on his secrets. Maybe he is planning to stop Zidar...or maybe he doesn't have the strength for it?"

Astra and Zoe looked around at the beautiful floating islands and the contented unicorns, tending to them.

"Everyone looks so happy," said Zoe, still unwilling to believe what Shadow was saying.

"Of course they do," replied Shadow. "Isn't this what everyone wants – to be master of their own little worlds, believing in their own magical powers?"

"But after all your lies, how do I know

you're telling us the truth?" demanded Astra.

"You'll have to work it out for yourself," Shadow replied carelessly. "But remember – the longer you stay here, the weaker your magic will become. And then, you'll never be able to escape."

Astra turned to Zoe. "There's only one way to find out if we are under Zidar's magic – and that's to cast an Unravelling Spell. I'll say it for both of us. We'll need to stand very still. Are you ready?"

Zoe felt a great sense of sadness. If all this was an illusion, then she never really had any magic at all. But, above all, she needed to know the truth.

"Go ahead," she whispered. "Cast the spell."

Astra nodded and began to chant:

Strip back the magic, lay it bare,
Show us the truth now, if you dare.
No illusions! No false promise!
Keep it true and keep it honest...

As Astra chanted the last words of the spell, Zoe let out a startled gasp as they took effect. For now, for the first time, they could see the Floating Islands for what they were – just pieces of empty rock.

"So you were telling the truth!" said Zoe, looking over at Shadow.

"For once...yes," said Shadow, his face not

showing any emotion.

"What shall we do now, Astra?" asked Zoe. "We came for the Golden Orb, remember?"

"I know," said Astra. "But first we must help the other fairy unicorns – they're all trapped by Zidar's spell! There's no sign of him now. I don't know where he's gone but we have to free as many of these unicorns as we can, before he returns."

"Very heroic," muttered Shadow, but Astra didn't stop to listen to him. Instead, she flew from island to island, casting her Unravelling Spell.

Zoe watched her go. She saw how each fairy unicorn in turn gasped and stumbled in confusion, as the islands were revealed for what they really were.

When all the unicorns had been freed, Astra gathered them together. They hovered in a circle around her, listening as she told them of the trap. Some didn't want to believe it. Others were already burning in anger at what Zidar had done to them.

While the unicorns talked among themselves, Shadow called Astra back to them. "Now it's time for you to complete your mission – what you came here to do. You must find the Golden Orb. It lies in the centre of the islands, where the golden glow is at its brightest."

Astra and Zoe exchanged glances, both knowing what the other was thinking. *How could they trust Shadow, after all this time? And why was he suddenly so keen to help them?*

But Zoe knew there wasn't time to find out. She wasn't sure where Zidar had gone but, at any moment, he could be back, and they needed the Orb. Or rather, she admitted to herself, the King needed it.

"I know you don't trust me," said Shadow. "But, remember, I am powerless. I can't fight Zidar myself for the Orb – and that means I can't fight you either."

"Astra," said Zoe. "Shadow's right, and we're running out of time. We have to try and get the Orb, before it's too late. For the King," she added in a whisper.

Astra nodded in agreement. Then she turned to the other unicorns. "Who here wants to defeat Zidar?" she asked.

They all let out a cheer.

"Then we must fly together, towards the golden light. There we'll find the Golden Orb. If we can get the Orb, we'll defeat Zidar."

Zoe climbed onto Astra's back and they began to fly.

When Zoe turned, she saw the others were following, their eyes fixed on the golden light ahead, a beating army of wings.

"There!" Zoe cried, pointing. "I can see the Orb, Astra!"

It was a beautiful golden ball, like a miniature sun, just as she had imagined it. "We're so close, now," said Zoe.

But before they could reach it, Zidar swept down from above, shining almost brighter than the Orb, blinding them with his glowing light.

"Not so fast," he said. "You may have freed those unicorns, Astra, but they can't fight me. I have taken their powers. They are weak, useless, just like Shadow... You'll never be able to take the Orb from me."

"I'll fight you for it alone, then," said Astra.

Zidar just laughed. "You're nothing but a weak little unicorn. You'll never manage it."

Zoe could see from Astra's expression that she believed him – that she was doubting her own powers.

"What is it, Astra?" she said.

"I know I'm not weak," Astra whispered back. "But Zidar has been feeding on other unicorns' powers for so long, I'm not sure I *can* beat him."

Zoe turned to Shadow, who was now hovering at their side. "Are you going to help us?" she asked. "Or did you bring us here just so Zidar could defeat Astra?"

"There's only one way to stop Zidar," Shadow replied in a low murmur. "But I'm not going to tell you what it is. Astra came for the Orb, didn't she? And she will only be worthy of it if she can work out how to get it by herself."

Chapter Six

Zoe and Astra hovered in the air. Zoe was aware of the other unicorns behind them, awaiting Astra's lead, and Shadow beside them, looking at Astra through narrowed eyes. It was as if he was trying to work out if she had any chance of succeeding, and more than anything, Zoe wanted Astra to prove herself to him.

"Well," said Zidar, his voice more of a snarl now, all pretence gone. "Are you going to try and fight me for the Orb, or not? Because if not, you and your little human friend might as well go home."

And that's when Zoe saw the change in Astra – her eyes lit up, the stars on her coat began to shine, and she just knew Astra had worked out a way.

Beneath her breath, so Zidar couldn't hear her, Astra began to mutter a spell.

That Golden Orb, a tiny sun,
Double up, be more than one!
Two Golden Orbs, shining bright,
Now who can tell, which one is right?

Zoe watched in wonder as another, identical, Golden Orb appeared in the sky.

"You've created an illusion?" she whispered to Astra.

"Yes," Astra replied, smiling. "That's how Zidar tricked us. And that's how I'm going to trick him."

Astra swished her horn one way, then the other, and the Orbs began to spin around each other, faster and faster, until it was impossible to tell which was which, except that one seemed to be glowing brighter than the other.

"I won't fight you for the Orb, Zidar," said Astra. "But I'll set you this challenge, if you'll accept. Which is the real Orb? You choose... and I'll take the other."

Zidar smiled and Zoe could tell from his expression that he'd never be able to resist the challenge. He circled the Orbs, fluttering round them, examining them closely, while Astra held her breath. All they could do was wait, tensely, while he decided. At last, he nodded, horn lowered.

"I choose this one as my Orb," said Zidar.

Astra shrugged, as if it meant nothing to her. "Then we'll take the other," she said.

As she spoke, she flew beside it and Zoe reached out, grasping it in her hands, amazed that something so small could shine

 so brightly. Even
as she touched it,
she knew they had
the right one,
though it was
almost as light as air
in her hands. She could sense its power
flooding through her; she could feel it fizzing
and humming with magic.

As soon as Zoe held it safely in her arms,
Astra cried out, "Now, everyone, to Unicorn
Island! Follow me!"

Then she turned tail, streaking through
the sky like a falling arrow. Shadow was
beside them, his powerful wings beating in
unison with Astra's, while the other unicorns
followed close behind.

"Well done, Astra," Shadow murmured.

"But Zidar's already giving chase," said Zoe, glancing over her shoulder. "Will the other unicorns be able to keep up with us? Hasn't Zidar stolen their magic?"

"Their magic, yes," said Astra, "but not their ability to fly."

"But Unicorn Island is a long way," said Zoe. "If Zidar is as powerful as he says he is, he'll easily catch us and take back the Orb. Should we take the Sky Lift? Maybe if we reached it first..."

Shadow shook his head. "The Sky Lift only takes you up, not down," he said. "Zoe's right, however. Zidar is already gaining on us. What are you going to do now, Astra?"

He said the words challengingly, as if once

again he was testing Astra, to see what she was made of.

Zoe turned again, to see Zidar's face set and grim. Astra had only brought them a few moments' lead when she tricked him with the illusion. Astra, too, looked back in alarm. "We'll never be able to out-fly him. And I can tell he's already muttering spells to try and stop us from escaping. I've got to defend the Orb and protect the other unicorns..."

"*Use* the Orb, Astra!" urged Zoe. "Isn't it meant to give you strength?"

"Of course," said Astra. "Why didn't I think of that? I must have panicked."

For a moment, Astra shut her eyes, feeling the strength and the power of the Orb. "It's as if I can speak to it," she told Zoe, "or as if it's speaking to me."

She began murmuring, asking the Orb to restore the powers of the other unicorns, and to give them all strength and speed.

As she spoke, the Orb began to shimmer, spreading its golden glow around them – Zoe and Astra, Shadow and all the fairy unicorns. It was like a shimmering net, stretching out to the last of the unicorns flying in their wake.

"Zidar!" Zoe called, watching him closely. "He's about to attack!"

His horn was lowered and he was aiming it at the slowest unicorns, knowing Astra would turn back to protect them.

But before he could strike, the golden net

began fizzing and sparkling, filling the air
with hundreds of tiny golden stars.

Zoe could feel its power and warmth
seeping through her, and as one, Astra,
Shadow and the other unicorns began to
plummet through the sky, faster and faster,
like a fiery comet heading straight for
Unicorn Island. In a moment, Zidar was left
far behind.

"You'll regret this, Astra!" he called after
them, his face full of fury.

But his words were soon whipped away as

they swept through the skies.

"Will he try to come after us?" Zoe asked, looking across at Shadow.

"He won't dare come to Unicorn Island," Shadow replied. "Not after everyone finds out what he's done."

When Zoe turned back she could already see Unicorn Island coming into view, a lush green landscape surrounded by azure sea.

"How could I ever have thought the Floating Islands were more beautiful than this?" she wondered.

Astra began chanting another spell, this time to still their speed.

"Watch out, everyone!" she cried. "Coming in to land!"

The unicorns spread their wings wide to slow their fall, and they touched down with a gentle bump in the Flower Meadows, in a cloud of sweet-scented petals.

"You did it!" said Zoe, flinging her arms around Astra's neck.

"*We* did it," Astra replied, blushing, as all the other unicorns came forward to thank her.

"Who knows for how long we could have been trapped there?" said one unicorn. "You rescued us. For that, we will always be grateful, Astra."

"I was happy to help," Astra replied. Then

she looked over at Shadow. "And, I have to admit, you owe your thanks to Shadow, too. He was the one who told us what Zidar was up to."

Shadow's eyes gleamed, as if knowing how much it cost Astra to thank him.

"One question," said Zoe, turning to Astra. "How did you know Zidar would choose the wrong Orb?"

"I know exactly what Astra did," interjected Shadow, laughing. "She simply made her Orb shine brighter than the real one. You knew that Zidar was greedy, so you were sure he'd go for the brightest Orb..."

"That's exactly it," said Astra, finding herself smiling back at Shadow. "Sometimes it's the simplest solution that solves the most difficult problem."

Then she took a deep breath.

"And now," she said, "it's time to take the Orb to the King."

"I'll come with you," said Shadow. "This should be interesting."

"What do you mean?" asked Astra, but Shadow just shook his head.

Zoe picked up the Orb, clasping it in her arms again. Then she swung herself onto Astra's back and they flew up to the castle entrance, Shadow by their side. The gates to the castle were wide open, and they trotted through the courtyard and made their way straight to the throne room. It felt so strange, Zoe thought, returning like this with their old enemy, and she could see all the

fairy unicorns they passed staring at them
in shock.

When they reached the throne room, Astra
knocked on the door.

"Come in!" called the King.

They entered to see the King flanked by
five of the Guardians – Lily, Sorrel, Eirra,
Nimbus and Medwen.

"Your Majesty," said Astra, gesturing to Zoe

beside her. "Look what we've brought you..."

And Zoe held out the Orb. It floated from
her hands, unbidden,
and hung in the air
above the King,
lighting the room
with its glow.

The King just stared at
it for a moment, and then at
Astra, and finally, at
Shadow. "I can't believe it,"
he said. "At last, it has been
revealed. Guardians...greet the next
ruler of Unicorn Island!"

Chapter Seven

There was a collective gasp as Shadow
stepped forward, giving a low chuckle,
clearly enjoying the moment.

"Don't panic," he drawled. "The King
certainly doesn't mean *me*."

"Then who?" asked Lily, Guardian of
the Flowers.

"Astra," replied the King.

"Astra?" repeated her mother, Sorrel, her voice tinged with disbelief.

"But she's so...young!" said Nimbus, Guardian of the Clouds.

Zoe and Astra both gazed at the King, shock on their faces. "How can it be me?" said Astra. "What are you talking about? I don't understand..."

"I told you long ago of a prophecy," said the King. "Do you remember? That a little unicorn and a human child would help save Unicorn Island. And that prophecy came to pass when you helped us to defeat Shadow. There is a Book of Prophecies, you see, passed down from one ruler to the next, kept safely here, within the castle walls. And it tells of other prophecies too. It tells how a ruler knows who to pass the crown onto when their time has come."

"But your time hasn't come yet!" insisted Zoe.

"It has," said the King. "I am older than I seem.

I have ruled Unicorn Island for many years
and I can feel that my powers are fading.
But that is no bad thing. I have many plans
for the future! I can explore the world
beyond Unicorn Island, free from the
responsibility of being King. And now the
moment has come to pass on my crown."

"T-t-to me?" stammered Astra, unable to
take it in. "Are you really saying *I* am the
next ruler of Unicorn Island?"

"Yes," smiled the King. "You set yourself
three challenges to become a Guardian. You
chose to bring me the Grimoire, the precious
spell book, then the Silver Chalice, to reveal
the future, and finally, the Golden Orb,
which brings strength and power. But that
makes you more than a Guardian, Astra. For

in the Book of Prophecies, it is written that
the unicorn who brings those three objects
will be the next King or Queen."

Zoe looked over at Astra, her eyes shining,
feeling nothing but pride in her friend.

"You are young, Astra," the King went on,
"but you are powerful, too. I was not much
older than you when I first became King.
And you have the Guardians to help you
and, of course, Zoe."

The King turned to the Guardians.
"Will you support Astra, and guide her?"

The Guardians all nodded. Then Zoe
looked over to see Shadow, standing a
little way apart from them all, and he was
nodding with them. As for Sorrel – her eyes
were brimming with tears as she stood beside

her daughter,
nuzzling her close.
"Can this
really be true?"
said Astra.

"It is," said the
King. And when Sorrel had left Astra's side,
he beckoned her over. "Zoe, come too," he
said. "Let's talk in private for a while."

"We'll arrange everything that needs to be
done for the ceremony," said Sorrel.

Then the King led Astra and Zoe through
a little door at the back of the throne room,
and into a smaller chamber.

As the door closed behind them, the last
thing Zoe saw was Shadow, watching them,
his expression inscrutable.

"I know this all seems very sudden, Astra," said the King. "But you are truly worthy of the crown. You have proved yourself over these past three challenges. I have been waiting for this moment, hoping you would bring me the Orb, unable to interfere. And I had already told the Guardians that I felt my time as King was drawing to a close."

For a moment, Astra seemed lost for words. "But what about the Guardians?" she said. "I still feel it should be one of them."

"Astra," said the King gently. "You know our customs. The prophecy must be fulfilled. You are the chosen one." He paused for a moment and looked at her, deep into her eyes. "That is, if you want to be, of course. Will you accept the crown?"

Astra nodded, looking back at the King. "I will," she said.

At those words, the King smiled. "I'll stay on the island at first, to guide you. You won't have to do this alone."

"I'll be there for you, Astra," said Zoe, "whenever I can."

Astra smiled at her gratefully.

"But there's just one thing I don't understand," Zoe went on. "Can we trust Shadow? At first, I thought he wanted the Golden Orb for himself, to get his powers back, but instead he helped us. Has he *really* changed? I can't quite believe it."

"The spell I cast over Shadow, to take away his powers, means he has no way of getting them back," explained the King, "even if he possessed the Golden Orb. Shadow knew this, and I expect he knew of the prophecy too. The Book of Prophecies should only have been read by the ruler, but it would be just like Shadow to have found a way to read it."

"So he really did come to the Floating Islands to help us?" said Zoe.

"Perhaps," said Astra, slowly, "or maybe if Shadow knew I might be the next ruler, he just wanted me on his side. Perhaps he thinks he'll be able to control me?"

"Who knows?" said the King. "You can never really tell with Shadow. But he is clever and knowledgeable – powerful even without magic. My advice would be to keep him close – then you can keep an eye on him."

Astra nodded. "I'll do that," she said. "I feel as if I have a lot to learn."

"You will rise to the challenge," said the King, "I am sure of it. But now it is time to celebrate…"

The King led them out of the chamber, and then across the courtyard, strangely empty and quiet now. "We're heading for the Flower Meadows," said the King, as they took flight over the tumbling waterfall.

Zoe looked up to see the skies were filled with fairy unicorns. They were coming from all over the island, answering the Guardians' call. There were Cloud Unicorns and Flower Unicorns, Unicorns of the Woods and Forests, and River Unicorns, too, rising up from the Moon River.

"Oh Astra!" said Zoe. "They've all come to see you crowned queen."

Astra, Zoe and the King landed at the edge of the Flower Meadows, near the Rose Bower. And when everyone had gathered, the King began to chant a spell beneath his breath. His crown rose into the air, hovered above him for a moment and then gently lowered itself into Zoe's hands.

"Zoe," said the King, smiling at her, "will you do the honours?"

Zoe grinned. "I'd love to," she said.

Then the King turned to the other unicorns.

"I present to you your new ruler," he said, his voice solemn, but full of pride. "My time has come, and Astra has proved herself worthy of the crown."

He looked over at Zoe then, and nodded.
Slowly, and carefully, Zoe placed the crown
on Astra's head.

There was a moment of silence, and then the
fairy unicorns broke into whoops and cheers.

Their hooves pummelled the ground in a grand applause, but loudest of all came Sorrel's voice, celebrating her daughter.

The golden crown cast dazzling rays around Astra, and Zoe gazed at her in wonder. "My friend," she whispered. "Queen of Unicorn Island."

Then, one by one, the Guardians came over to congratulate Astra, followed by Shadow. And then came Tio, beaming at her. "Well done, Astra," he said. "I'll always be here, at your side."

"Thank you, Tio," said Astra. She bent her head to whisper to Tio and Zoe. "I still can't quite believe it!"

"I know you're going to be a brilliant queen," said Zoe. "And I'm sorry, too, if I let you down when we were on our island. I so wanted to believe that I had magic too."

"But you do," said Astra. "Because of our connection, some of my magic has become yours. And I never could have done any of this without you. It was you who gave me the confidence to believe in myself – back when I was a little unicorn without any magic at all. Do you remember?"

Zoe hesitated for a moment. Wearing the crown made Astra seem older, somehow, and different. But when she looked into Astra's eyes she saw everything her friend was feeling – her pride, and her fear, too – and she leaned over and gave Astra a hug.

"Now," said the King, "it's time for the party to begin!"

He flew above the meadows, casting spells that lit the darkening sky with fireworks. Below, tables appeared, groaning with delicious food, and music filled the air.

Zoe feasted and
danced, chatting and
laughing with the fairy
unicorns.

And as the party drew to a close, Astra and Zoe found each other again, by the silvery waters of Moon River.

"Time for me to go home," said Zoe, sadly.

Astra knelt down, Zoe swung herself onto Astra's back one last time, and they flew together to the Great Oak.

Astra set her down by the entrance.

"I'll be back," said Zoe, "as soon as I can. Only...won't you be too busy, now that you're Queen?"

"I'll always have time for you," promised Astra. "Never doubt that, Zoe."

Zoe hugged her friend and turned to go, but Astra called her back. "I thought finding

the Golden Orb might be our last
challenge, our last big adventure,"
she said. "But really, Zoe, our biggest
adventure is about to begin..."

Designed by Brenda Cole

Edited by Lesley Sims

With thanks to Alison Kelly

First published in 2022 by Usborne Publishing Ltd., Usborne House,
83-85 Saffron Hill, London EC1N 8RT, England. usborne.com
Copyright © 2022 Usborne Publishing Ltd.